Eleanor the Snow White Fairy

To Erin, from the fairies

ORCHARD BOOKS
338 Euston Road, London NW1 3BH
Orchard Books Australia
Level 17/207 Kent Street, Sydney, NSW 2000
A Paperback Original

First published in 2015 by Orchard Books

A CIP catalogue record for this book is available from the British Library.

ISBN 978 1 40833 673 1

5 7 9 10 8 6

Printed and bound by CPI Group (UK) Ltd, Croydon, CR0 4YY

The paper and board used in this book are natural recyclable products made from wood grown in responsibly managed forests.

Orchard Books is an imprint of Hachette Children's Group and published by The Watts Publishing Group Limited, an Hachette UK company.

www.hachette.co.uk

Eleanor the Snow White Fairy

by Daisy Meadows

ORCHARD

www.rainbowmagic.co.uk

The Fairyland Palace
Fairytale Lane
Rachel's House
Tippington Town

Jack Frost's
Ice Castle
Forest
Tiptop Castle

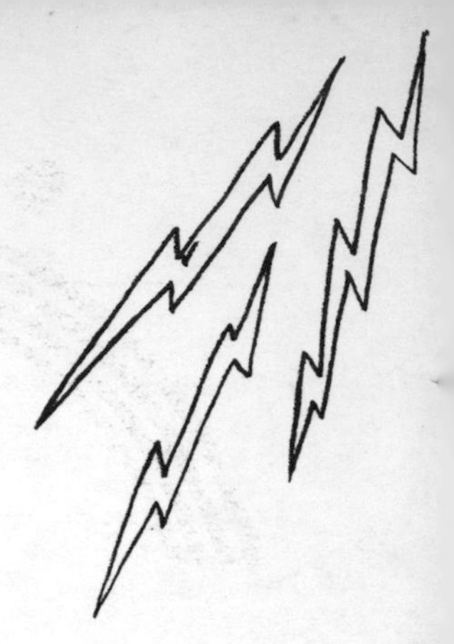

Jack Frost's Spell

The Fairytale Fairies are in for a shock!
Cinderella won't run at the strike of the clock.
No one can stop me – I've plotted and planned,
And I'll be the fairest Ice Lord in the land.

It will take someone handsome and witty and clever
To stop storybook endings for ever and ever.
But to see fairies suffer great trouble and strife,
Will make me live happily all of my life!

Contents

Chapter One:	A Surprise Reflection	9
Chapter Two:	Too Many Dwarves	21
Chapter Three:	The Magic Comb	33
Chapter Four:	The Vainest of Them All	45
Chapter Five:	The Prettiest in the Land	55
Chapter Six:	A Fairytale Picnic	65

A Surprise Reflection

When Kirsty Tate opened her eyes, for a moment she couldn't remember where she was. She gazed up at the canopy that hung over her four-poster bed. A spring breeze had wafted open the gauzy curtains, and the sun lit up the white dressing table with its gold and silver swirls. On the dressing table lay a book with a sparkling cover – *The Fairies' Book of Fairy Tales.*

A smile spread across Kirsty's face as she remembered everything that had happened the day before. She sat up and looked across to where her best friend, Rachel Walker, was still fast asleep.

"Rachel, wake up," she said in a gentle voice. "It's our second day at Tiptop Castle!"

Rachel opened her eyes and gave Kirsty a sleepy smile. They were staying in a beautiful old castle on the outskirts of Tippington, where the Fairytale Festival was being held. Their bedroom was at the top of a tower of the castle, and the girls had agreed that it was fit for a princess – or two!

"What are you going to wear today?" asked Kirsty, hopping out of bed and opening the enormous wardrobe where they had hung their clothes.

"How about our fairy dresses?" suggested Rachel, swinging her legs out of bed. "It'd be fun to join in with everyone else."

The day before, all the festival organisers had been wearing fairytale fancy dress. Kirsty clapped her hands together.

"That's a great idea," she said, "especially after our Fairyland visit yesterday!"

As they pulled on their beautiful fairy dresses, they talked about the adventure they had shared with Julia the Sleeping Beauty Fairy.

After meeting Hannah the Happy Ever After Fairy in the reading room of the castle, she had whisked them to Fairyland and introduced them to the Fairytale Fairies. Julia the Sleeping Beauty Fairy, Eleanor the Snow White Fairy, Faith the Cinderella Fairy and Lacey the Little Mermaid Fairy had presented them with the beautiful *Fairies' Book of Fairy Tales.* But when they opened the book, the pages were blank. Jack Frost had stolen the fairies' magical objects, and now he had the power to rewrite the fairy tales to be about him and the goblins. The fairytale characters had fallen out of their stories and were lost in the human world, along with the magical objects.

"I'm so happy that we managed to

help Julia to get her magical jewellery box back," said Rachel.

"And Sleeping Beauty and her prince are back in their story," Kirsty added. "But we have to do the same for the other fairies. They need their objects to look after their fairy tales."

She smiled as Rachel pulled on her mini backpack with its glittery fairy wings. It was funny to wear false wings because they knew how it felt to have real ones!

"I wonder if we'll meet any of our fairy

friends today," said Rachel. "Perhaps they've already managed to find their magical objects."

She walked over to the dressing table and picked up *The Fairies' Book of Fairy Tales.* They had read it together last night, and the pink-ribbon bookmark was still in the first story – *Sleeping Beauty.*

When Julia had got her magical jewellery box back, the first story had returned to the sparkly covered book. Kirsty peered over Rachel's shoulder as she turned to the second story, *Snow White*. But the pages were still blank.

"It looks as if Jack Frost still has the other three magical objects," said Kirsty, as Rachel flicked through the blank pages of the rest of the book.

"Then we just have to get them back before the Fairytale Festival is spoiled," said Rachel in a determined voice. "But first we need to do each other's hair, right?"

"Right!" said Kirsty with a giggle.

They decorated each other's hair with glittery Alice bands, hair bobbles and clips.

"The perfect finishing touch to our fairy outfits," said Rachel, looking at Kirsty with a smile. "Is there a mirror? I want to show you what I've done!"

She looked around and saw a hand mirror lying on the dressing table. There were intricate carvings of birds and butterflies in the dark-wood frame and handle, and the glass was old but beautifully polished. Rachel held it up so that Kirsty could see her reflection.

"How do you think I look?" Kirsty asked.

Rachel opened her mouth to reply, but before she could speak a silvery voice came from the mirror.

"Although you are pretty and ever so sweet,

Snow White is the loveliest you'll ever meet!"

Too Many Dwarves

The girls stared at the mirror in amazement.

"It's a talking mirror," said Kirsty. "I've never seen anything like it!"

"But you've read about it," said Rachel, suddenly excited. "We both have – in the story of *Snow White*!"

She turned the mirror around and looked into it. Her reflection gazed back at her. Feeling a little shy, Rachel cleared her throat.

"How do I look?" she asked.

At once, the silvery voice spoke again.

"Although you're much fairer than many I've seen,

Snow White has more beauty than you or the queen."

Rachel and Kirsty laughed and gazed into the mirror together.

"I'd love to see the real Snow White," said Kirsty. "She must be incredibly beautiful."

"She is," said a tinkling voice behind them.

"Look!" Rachel exclaimed.

In the mirror they could see the

reflection of a tiny fairy fluttering behind them.

"It's Eleanor the Snow White Fairy!" said Kirsty, whirling around. "Hello, Eleanor!"

Smiling, Eleanor flcw over to land on the dressing table. Her swishy lilac dress swirled out around her and her lovely dark fringe was set off perfectly by her yellow Alice band.

"Good morning, Rachel and Kirsty," she said. "I see you've found the magic mirror."

"Is it really the one from the fairy tale?" Rachel asked.

"Yes, and I'm very glad to know where it is," said Eleanor, giving the mirror a little pat. "But all the characters are still lost, and the story will be ruined forever if I don't get back my magical jewelled hair comb."

"We'll help you to find Jack Frost and the goblins," Kirsty promised. "Hide in my backpack and we'll go downstairs and start searching."

Eleanor flew into Kirsty's backpack while Rachel tucked the magic mirror inside hers. Then they left their tower-top room and hurried down the winding stairs towards the main castle. Halfway down, they saw a girl dressed as Little Red Riding Hood.

"Hello!" called the girls as they dashed past her.

Little Red Riding Hood waved, but Rachel and Kirsty had already disappeared around the next bend. Next they saw a boy dressed as Jack from *Jack and the Beanstalk*.

"Morning!" called the girls as they clattered down the remaining steps and reached the corridor.

Jack just stared after them with his mouth open. Kirsty and Rachel giggled as they ran down the corridor.

"Why did he look so surprised?" asked Kirsty.

"Perhaps he's never seen a fairy before," said Rachel, pointing at her wings with a laugh.

Just then, they heard loud noises of clattering, clanging and shouting.

"It's coming from the castle kitchens," Kirsty exclaimed. "Come on, let's go and find out what's wrong."

It didn't take them long to reach the kitchens. They burst through the doors and stared in astonishment at the scene of chaos. A beautiful young woman was trying to pack a picnic, surrounded by dwarves. Some of them were juggling with the boiled eggs, bowling with the apples and trying to balance the sandwiches on their noses.

"Please, dwarves," said the young woman in a gentle voice. "You're really not helping – don't you *want* a nice picnic?"

"Yes – we want it right now!" squawked one of the dwarves.

He rammed some grapes into his mouth and chewed them with his mouth open.

"What bad manners!" Rachel exclaimed.

"They're not normally so rude to me," said the young woman, sounding upset. "We share a little cottage and they're usually very sweet."

"Oh my goodness, said Kirsty. "Are you Snow White?"

"Yes, how did you know?" Snow White asked.

"There's only one beautiful princess who shares a cottage with lots of dwarves," Kirsty replied, smiling. "But I thought there were only seven of them?"

"That's right," said Snow White, sounding surprised.

"But there are more than seven dwarves here," said Rachel. "Excuse me, everyone, would you all line up so that we can count you?"

After a lot of shoving, shuffling and grumbling, the dwarves were standing in a very uneven line. Kirsty, Rachel and Snow White walked along and counted them.

"Eleven," said Kirsty.

"There can't be!" said Snow White. "Let's count them again."

But halfway along the line, one of the

dwarves stuck out his foot and Rachel tripped over it. She landed on her knees and let out a cry.

"Ha ha, enjoy your trip?" asked the dwarf.

Kirsty looked down and saw that the dwarf who had tripped her up had enormous feet. So did the dwarf next to him – and the next two as well. They were all sniggering, and Kirsty recognised the sneering sound very well.

"Those aren't dwarves!" she cried, pulling Rachel to her feet. "They're goblins!"

The Magic Comb

"RUN!" bawled the goblins.

They burst out through the kitchen door into the garden, and Kirsty pelted after them, dragging Rachel behind her. They raced along gravel paths, past elegant hedges and statues. Eleanor peeped out of Kirsty's backpack as they sprinted along.

"They're heading towards the forest!" she cried. "You'll never catch them on foot. Let me turn you into fairies – it'll be quicker if we can all fly!"

Panting, the girls dived behind a high hedge and Eleanor sprang out of the backpack. She held up her wand and waved it over Rachel and Kirsty. There was a dazzling flash of silver light, and when the sparkles cleared, Rachel and Kirsty were hovering in the air beside Eleanor.

Their pretend wings had disappeared and been replaced by real gauzy fairy wings, and their fairy dresses were floating around them.

"The goblins have already disappeared into the forest," said Eleanor. "Come on – we can catch them if we hurry!"

Together, they zoomed into the forest and zipped through the trees, but there was no sign of the goblins. Eleanor swooped down and the girls followed her, looking for any sign that the goblins had passed that way. Then Rachel gave a shout.

"Look – a print!"

She pointed down at an enormous footprint in the mud.

"That's definitely a goblin footprint," said Kirsty, looking at the splayed-out toes. "Are there more? Perhaps we could track them."

"Yes, over here!" called Eleanor, spotting another one.

The fairies flew on, following the trail of footprints through the muddiest part of the undergrowth. After a few minutes, they heard voices – cackling, squabbling voices.

"Those are goblins," said Rachel. "We must be close."

"I think there's a clearing up ahead," said Eleanor, who was in the lead. "Let's be careful."

They flew slowly and tucked themselves into a bushy plant before peeping out into the clearing. Sure enough, the four goblins were there – still disguised as dwarves. They were standing beside a large pile of logs, looking cross and confused.

"Look – there's Jack Frost!" exclaimed Kirsty.

The Ice Lord was sitting on a stool beside a small pond. He was combing his hair and beard, and admiring his reflection in the water. As the fairies watched, he half turned and glared at the goblins.

"Why are you all standing there like lemons?" he demanded. "Get on with it! I want a cottage and I want it NOW."

"But we've never built a cottage before," wailed the tallest of the goblins. "We don't know how!"

"That's not my problem," said Jack Frost. "I want it to look just like Snow White's cottage, only *better*. Stop being so lazy and start building!"

"Let's get closer," whispered Rachel.

She flew out of the plant and up to the leafy branches of a tree above the pond. Kirsty and Eleanor followed her, and they all looked down through the leaves at Jack Frost.

"I'm the prettiest in the land," Jack was saying to himself in a sing-song voice. "There's no one as pretty as me, not even Snow White!"

Suddenly, Eleanor gasped and almost fell off her branch. She had to flutter her wings to steady herself.

"What is it?" Kirsty asked in a low voice.

"Look what he's using to comb his hair," Eleanor whispered. "It's my magical jewelled comb!"

The girls peered down at the delicate comb in Jack Frost's hand. It was shaped like a tiny silver bow, and decorated with shimmering pearls.

"We've found it," said Rachel with a relieved sigh. "Now we just have to figure out a way to get it back."

They all thought hard as Jack Frost continued to preen himself, smiling and nodding at his watery reflection.

"There's no one as lovely as me," he murmured. "Everyone is jealous of me, and so they should be!"

"I've got an idea," said Kirsty. "He's the vainest person I've ever met, and I think we could use that to help us get the comb back. Eleanor, could you turn me and Rachel into goblins?"

Eleanor nodded, and the three friends fluttered down to hide behind the tree. Rachel handed Eleanor the magic mirror for safekeeping, and then a swift flick of her fairy wand transformed Rachel and Kirsty into warty goblins. They couldn't help but giggle as they looked at each other. They looked so funny as goblins!

"Come on," Kirsty said. "We have to convince Jack Frost to hand over the comb, and I think I know how!"

The Vainest of Them All

In their goblin disguises, Rachel and Kirsty stomped across the clearing towards Jack Frost. He scowled when he saw them.

"Go and help the others build my cottage," he demanded.

"But we just wanted to tell you something," said Kirsty quickly.

"Well?" Jack Frost snapped. "What is it?"

"Just that you are so handsome," said Kirsty. "Your hair is beautifully spiky and your beard is as icy and shiny as fresh snow."

Jack Frost couldn't help but give a proud smile. He stroked his beard and puffed out his chest.

"I *am* magnificent," he agreed. "Carry on. More praise!"

"No one could look more wonderful than

you," said Rachel. "Oh please, may we have the honour of combing your beard for you?"

"No way," said Jack Frost, tightening his grip on the comb. "Goblins always tug too hard. You'll pull my hair out by the roots!"

"We'll be careful," Kirsty promised.

But Jack Frost shook his head.

"I can comb it better myself," he said. "You lot can't make it look pretty enough."

Rachel and Kirsty exchanged worried looks. Then a different idea popped into Rachel's head.

"I know where's there's a lovely mirror," she said in a boastful voice. "You could see yourself much better than in the pond reflection. I could get it for you – if you'd let me have the comb as a reward."

"I want that mirror, but I'm not giving you the comb," Jack Frost screeched. "Get me the mirror! Don't be so greedy!"

Rachel and Kirsty didn't dare to argue with him any more.

They backed away, and Jack Frost returned to gazing at his own reflection. The girls hurried behind the tree in their goblin disguises, and found Eleanor waiting for them.

"I'm sorry," said Kirsty, looking crestfallen. "I really thought my idea could work."

"It's OK," said Eleanor. "It was a good try. We'll just have to think of something else."

They all stared at each other, but they couldn't think of a single plan.

Then they heard the sound of branches cracking and plants being crushed underfoot. A shrill voice was shouting something, and they all listened hard as the noise grew louder. Someone was crashing through the forest towards the clearing, and they sounded very angry. After a few seconds, the fairies were able to make out the words.

"Where's my magic mirror?" the high-pitched voice was screaming. "Give me my magic mirror!"

The voice sent shivers down the girls' backs.

"Who could it be?" asked Kirsty in a whisper.

"It's the wicked queen," said Eleanor. "She's Snow White's stepmother, and she's obsessed with staring into the mirror because she's so terribly vain. She always asks it the same question."

"She wants to know 'Who is the prettiest of them all?', doesn't she?" asked Rachel, remembering the story. "And one day the mirror starts saying 'Snow White', and the wicked queen is furious."

Eleanor nodded, and Kirsty gave a little cry of excitement.

"I know!" she said. "Eleanor, can you use your magic to make the mirror say Jack Frost's name?"

"Yes, I think so," said Eleanor. "But how will that help?"

"Because if *we* can't make Jack Frost give up the mirror, perhaps the wicked queen can," Kirsty explained. "She sounds pretty scary!"

Eleanor waved her wand over the mirror and spoke the words of a spell.

"We need to save my magic comb.
Please help us and you'll soon be home.
Instead of mentioning Snow White,
Declare Jack Frost the prettiest sight."

The mirror sparkled, and the three fairies looked at each other.

"Now we have to get Jack Frost to look into it," said Kirsty.

"That should be easy," said Rachel, standing up. "There's nothing he likes better than looking at himself."

"Bring me my magic mirror!" screamed the voice of the wicked queen.

She was very close now, and it seemed to the girls that even the leaves were shaking at the sound of her voice.

"Hurry, Rachel!" cried Eleanor. "She's almost here!"

The Prettiest in the Land

Just as the wicked queen pushed through the trees into the clearing, Rachel ran over to Jack Frost and held the mirror in front of his face. He gave an admiring 'oooh' of delight and started to comb his beard again.

"I'm so pretty!" he said, giving himself a loving smile.

At once, the silvery voice of the mirror spoke to him.

"Oh, fair Jack Frost, indeed it's true.

The prettiest in all the land is YOU!"

When he heard this, Jack Frost leapt to his feet and capered around the pond in delight.

"I'm the prettiest and the best!" he shouted. "I'm the prettiest and the – oh."

He spotted the wicked queen's shadow and stopped in his tracks. He looked slowly up at her face, and then his knees began to knock together.

Kirsty ran across to join Rachel, leaving Eleanor hovering beside the tree.

"She looks really scary," said Kirsty in Rachel's ear.

Clearly Jack Frost thought so too. He quivered as the queen glared at him. She was dressed in a swirling black cloak and wore a spiky silver crown. Her dark hair was threaded with white strands, and there were tiny lines around her eyes, but she was very beautiful. Then her mouth twisted into a snarl, and she didn't look beautiful any more.

"You're not the prettiest in the land!" she screeched. "It's me! Me, me, ME!"

She picked up her cloak and lunged towards Jack Frost, who gave a yell of fear and threw his hands into the air. The magical jewelled comb flew upwards and then fell towards the middle of the pond.

"I can't reach it!" cried Rachel as the comb went over their heads.

"But I can!" Eleanor called out, swooping away from the tree towards the pond.

With her hands outstretched, she managed to catch the comb just before it hit the water. It shrank to fairy size at once and Eleanor spun upwards, laughing with joy.

"My comb!" she exclaimed. "At last I can take it back where it belongs!"

Jack Frost was too busy cringing in front of the wicked queen to pay any attention to Eleanor.

"I'm sorry!" he whimpered. "You're right! Whatever you say – whatever you want – you're right!"

Eleanor fluttered down beside Rachel and Kirsty. A single touch of her wand transformed them into humans again, and they were once more wearing their fairy outfits and backpacks.

"My magical comb is safe, thanks to

you," Eleanor said. "It's time to return all things to their rightful owners."

She looked at the mirror, and then at the wicked queen.

"Of course," said Rachel, thinking of the *Snow White* fairy tale. "I had forgotten that the mirror belongs to the queen."

She walked slowly towards the angry queen, who was towering over Jack Frost.

"I'm right beside you," said Kirsty, slipping her hand into Rachel's hand.

"Excuse me?" said Rachel, feeling very nervous. "I think this belongs to you."

The queen turned her flashing eyes on Rachel, who held out the mirror. The queen snatched it, held it up and gazed at her reflection.

"Tell me the truth once and for all!" she shrieked. "Who is the prettiest in all the land?"

For a moment, everyone in the clearing held their breath.

"Snow White, of course," the mirror replied.

The wicked queen let out a squeal of rage…and then shimmered and faded back to her fairy tale.

A Fairytale Picnic

As the queen disappeared, the girls heard happy voices echoing from among the trees. Then the bushes parted and Snow White stepped into the clearing, followed by the seven dwarves. They were carrying a large picnic hamper, plates and bottles. Snow White gave a little skip of happiness when she saw Rachel and Kirsty.

"Thank you for your help!" she called to them, as the dwarves put the hamper down. Enjoy the picnic!"

The girls waved to her and then she and the dwarves shimmered and disappeared.

"They've returned to the fairy tale," said Eleanor, landing on Kirsty's shoulder. "Thanks to you both, Snow White and all the other characters are back where they belong."

"That's wonderful," said Kirsty. "Another happy ending."

"Not for everyone," said Rachel, looking across at Jack Frost.

He had slumped down on his stool and rested his chin in his hands. The goblins abandoned their half-built log cottage and gathered around him.

"Don't be sad," said the shortest goblin.

"You can yell at me if you want," said a very pimply goblin.

Jack Frost lifted his head and peered at his sad reflection in the pond. His bottom lip wobbled.

"I *am* the prettiest in the land," he muttered.

"You *are*!" shouted the goblins. "Of course you are! That Snow White isn't a patch on you."

"She didn't even have a beard," added the tallest goblin.

Jack Frost started to look a bit happier, and the girls grinned at each other.

"I think it's time for us to go back to the castle," said Rachel.

"And for me to return to Fairyland," said Eleanor. "Thank you for everything! I can't wait to tell the other fairies that another of our fairy tales is safe again!"

With a merry wave of her hand, she vanished back to Fairyland. Rachel and Kirsty looked down at the picnic hamper.

"Let's take this back with us," Kirsty suggested.

Together, they lifted the heavy basket and carried it back through the forest, along the gravel paths and past the elegant hedges and statues. By the time they reached the castle, they were feeling very hungry indeed. They saw a group of children sitting on the grass and waved. The children dressed as Red Riding Hood and Jack from *Jack and the Beanstalk* waved back at them.

"Look, there are the girl and boy we saw earlier," said Rachel. "I wonder if they'd like to share the picnic with us."

They went over to ask them, and they agreed happily. A short while later, all the children were sitting on a large picnic rug in the middle of the largest lawn. Rachel and Kirsty had quickly made a lot of new friends. Little Red Riding Hood's name was Emily, and

the boy dressed as Jack was called Omri. Everyone had enjoyed Snow White's wonderful picnic, and they were all full up and happy.

"Perhaps someone should tell a story," said Emily in a sleepy voice.

"We've got the perfect book upstairs," said Rachel, jumping to her feet. "I'll go and fetch it."

She ran into the castle and up the winding staircase to the tower bedroom. A few moments later she hurried back across the lawn and sat down with the other children.

"That was quick," said Kirsty.

"I ran all the way," Rachel panted, handing her the sparkling *Fairies' Book of Fairy Tales*. "You read it, Kirsty – I'm all out of breath."

Kirsty opened the book and turned to the second story. The words and pictures had returned, and she held up the pages to show Rachel. The girls shared a secret smile and then Kirsty started to read.

"Once upon a time there was a young princess called Snow White..."

Rachel turned the pages, and everyone listened, enchanted, as Kirsty read the story. When she finished, everyone clapped, but Rachel turned the next page and sighed. The following pages were still blank, and the girls exchanged a worried look.

"Two fairy tales are still missing," said Rachel in a low voice.

"And there are two more magical objects to find," Kirsty added. "Oh, Rachel, I wonder what our next fairytale adventure will be!"

Meet the Fairytale Fairies

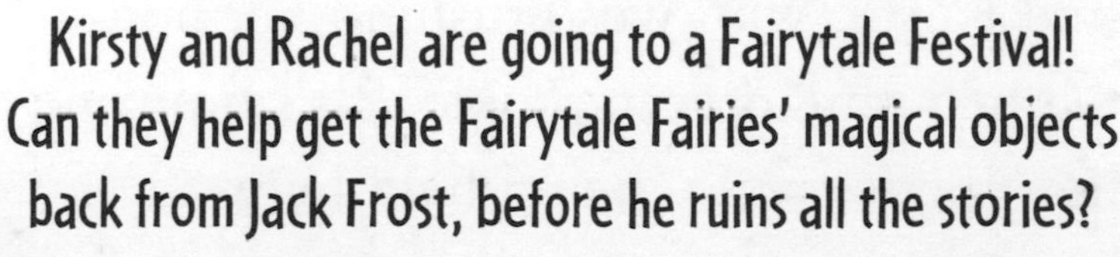

Kirsty and Rachel are going to a Fairytale Festival!
Can they help get the Fairytale Fairies' magical objects
back from Jack Frost, before he ruins all the stories?

www.rainbowmagicbooks.co.uk

Now it's time for Kirsty and Rachel to help...

Faith the Cinderella Fairy

Read on for a sneak peek...

"Another gorgeous day at Tiptop Castle!" exclaimed Rachel Walker, throwing open the window and breathing in the crisp morning air.

She was looking out of the tower-top bedroom that she was sharing with her best friend Kirsty Tate. They had been having a brilliant time at the Fairytale Festival, and they couldn't wait for this morning's ballroom-dancing lesson.

"I can't believe how lucky we are," said Kirsty, who was brushing her hair at the beautiful dressing table. "It's amazing that the festival is being held here, so close to Tippington – and we've made some great new friends."

Several children were staying at the castle, and there were fun fairytale activities to enjoy every day. Tippington was Rachel's home town, and Mrs Walker had arranged this special treat for them while Kirsty was staying during half term.

"It was so much fun dressing up yesterday," said Rachel, thinking of their fairy outfits. "I wonder what adventures today will bring!"

"Magical ones, I hope," said Kirsty with a happy smile.

On their first day at the castle, the girls had met their friend Hannah the Happy Ever After Fairy while they were exploring. They had shared many adventures in Fairyland, because they were good friends with the fairies, and they were thrilled when Hannah whisked them off to meet some very special fairies indeed. Julia the Sleeping Beauty Fairy, Eleanor the Snow White Fairy, Faith the Cinderella Fairy and Lacey the Little Mermaid Fairy were the Fairytale Fairies, and they gave the girls The Fairies' Book of s. It was a wonderful collection of the girls' four favourite s, but when they looked inside, the pages were blank.

Read **Faith the Cinderella Fairy** to find out what adventures are in store for Kirsty and Rachel!

Competition!

The Fairytale Fairies have created a special competition just for you!

Collect all four books in the Fairytale Fairies series and answer the special questions in the back of each one.

Once you have all the answers, take the first letter from each one and arrange them to spell a secret word! When you have the answer, go online and enter!

What is the name of the Jewellery-Making Fairy in the Magical Crafts Fairies series?

_ _ _ _ _

We will put all the correct entries into a draw and select a winner to receive a special Rainbow Magic Goody Bag featuring lots of treats for you and your fairy friends. You'll also feature in a new Rainbow Magic story!

Enter online now at www.rainbowmagicbooks.co.uk

No purchase required. Only one entry per child. Two prize draws will take place on 1st April 2015 and 2nd July 2015. Alternatively readers can send the answer on a postcard to:
Rainbow Magic, Fairytale Fairies Competition,
Orchard Books, 338 Euston Road, London, NW1 3BH. Australian readers can write to:
Rainbow Magic, Fairytale Fairies Competition, Hachette Children's Books,
level 17/207 Kent St, Sydney, NSW 2000. E-mail: childrens.books@hachette.com.au.
New Zealand readers should write to:
Rainbow Magic, Fairytale Fairies Competition,
PO Box 3255, Shortland St, Auckland 1140

Join in the magic online by signing up to the Rainbow Magic fan club!

Meet the fairies, play games and get sneak peeks at the latest books!

There's fairy fun for everyone at

www.rainbowmagicbooks.co.uk

You'll find great activities, competitions, stories and fairy profiles, and also a special newsletter.

Find a fairy with your name!